T0193278

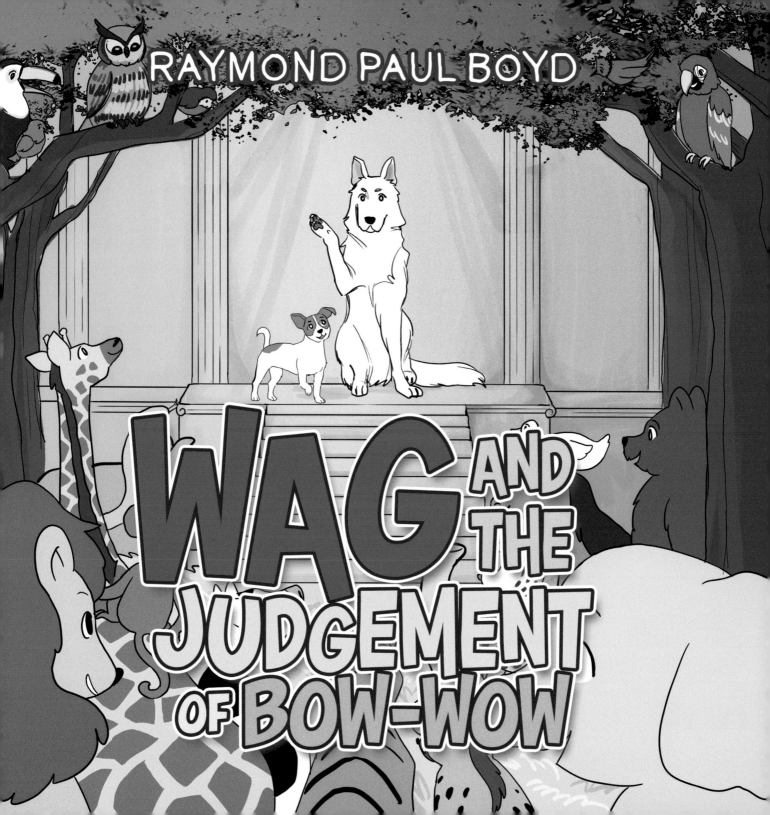

Copyright © 2022 by Raymond Paul Boyd. 831040

All rights reserved. No part of this book may be reproduced or
transmitted in any form or by any means, electronic or mechanical,
including photocopying, recording, or by any information storage and
retrieval system, without permission in writing from the copyright owner.

This is a work of fiction. Names, characters, places and incidents either
are the product of the author's imagination or are used fictitiously,
and any resemblance to any actual persons, living or dead, events, or
locales is entirely coincidental.

To order additional copies of this book, contact:
Xlibris
844-714-8691
www.Xlibris.com
Orders@Xlibris.com

ISBN: 978-1-6698-2728-3 (sc)
ISBN: 978-1-6698-2729-0 (e)

Print information available on the last page

Rev. date: 02/27/2023

Prologue

The enclosed narrative is written in the fervent wish to enlighten those of the adolescent age and the mental anguish. They cause their fellow human beings by their continuous bullying. Also the lesser of god's creatures have free will and a very small number of them bully those that are weak. This narrative is the telling of one of them namely Jaws the Pit-Bull.

Happily, and with curiosity every animal assembles once again in the great hall in the heavenly animal kingdom awaiting the arrival of the all-knowing Bow-wow. Having been summons by a single trumpet from ears the Bull Elephant. Wag, had taken his place on stage, he as the other had wonder what the all-knowing bow-wow was going to say?

There was not a need for any to wonder any longer as Bow-wow entered the great stage and was greeted with a thunder of applause. After a moment, Bow-wow smiled as he raised his right paw. The silence was instant even the flapping of wings of those that flew above remained suspended in mid-air as Bow-Wow begun to address the assemble saying "I sadly observed the blatant misbehavior of one of our brothers on earth". Therefore, I'm having our brother Wag to go to earth.

And have done with his misbehavior namely "Bullying". The offender is "Pit—Bull" better known by those he mistreats as "Jaws the Pit—bull".

Wag arrives on earth and observes that he's standing in front of a large sanctuary their animals of all kind are treated. Wag reads the sign above the door of the entrance. "All whom enters are cared for and loved". Attending Physician, Dr. Gloria Boyd.

First, mother Hound Dog tells of her 4 puppies having their large ears snapped at by that pesky Bull Dog.

Wag, enters the kennels adjacent to the hospital and listen to the second of complaints as told by mother cat. She tells of how jaws the Pit–Bull would offend snap at the tails of her 4 kittens as they play outdoors.

Wag then listen to a 6-month old female doe how her swiftness of foot saved her from the jaws of the Pit-bull.

Wag then listen to young Billy the goat. Tell how he had escaped from being bitten by Jaw's the Pit–Bull.

Next, snapper the turtle related the time Jaw's the Pit–bull tried to break his shell with his teeth in his attempt to do so he broke his tooth causing him to yap in pain as he ran away.

Wag, then listen to hoot the owl, tell of the day he had learn how to fly and that saved him from Jaw's trying to bit him.

Tails the Squirrel tell that his bushy tail had cause Jaw's the Pit—bull to choke when he attempted to bit it.

Quack, quack, mother Duck told how she and her 6 ducklings were barked at whenever they came out of the pond.

Next bald eagle whom was on the mend having suffered a broken left wing, Jaw's would annoy him as he sat on his perch dreaming of the day once again when he would soar happily again into the blue sky, adding that Jaw's the Pit—bull would no longer be able to jump up to reach his perch. He ceased only when I swatted him with my right wing. He then ran away.

Next, the mother of 2 French Poodles was anxious to tell of the time her 2 young ones were playfully engage in a game of a tug of war when Jaw's the Pit—bull bit the rope in half.

Wag then listen to the next complaint as told by mother rabbit of the day jaws the Pit—bull bit the ears of 2 of her 6 little ones.

Long neck the giraffe stepped forward and related on several occasion as he had been taking a nap Jaw's the Pit-bull would awaken him by barking loudly in his ear.

Wag determine the time had come to speak to Jaw's the Pit—bull as he was warming himself in the rays of the sun. Wag, asked why he misbehaved by bullying his sisters and brother? Jaws the Pit—bull replied with laughter that he was having fun.

Jaw's the Pit-bull ran off not paying attention to where he was going he didn't see that he was running towards the pond that was no longer frozen due to the warm rays of the sun. The thin coat of ice that covered the ponds deep cold-cold water broke as Jaw's the Pit-bull ran on it.

Wag, and those that express them complains with the exception of long neck the giraffe saw Jaw's the Pit–Bull trying to paw himself out. The doe and the squirrel ran to the pasture to tell long neck the Giraffe whom was munching on a bale of hay. They told of the plight of Jaw's the Pit–bull.

Whom now was begging to be rescued and to his surprise as he was about to drown in the freezing water, he felt himself being lifted by the scruff of his neck by long neck. The Giraffe to safety. Wag, then asked the shivering Jaw's the Pit—bull did he still wish to have fun being a Bully? He tearfully replied saying that he was sorry for having been a bully. Wag, smiled and said from this day forward you shall no longer be called Jaw's the Pit—bull but our big brother the Pit—bull. All shouted—Hooray! Hooray!

Wag, returned to the animal's heavenly kingdom he was greeted by the all-knowing bow-Wow and all the other that had gather in the "Animals heavenly kingdom" Bow-wow thanked him for doing a job well done. Wag in response ask what is my next assignment?

THE END?

Bullying is a crime against humanity, unfortunately it is committed by a segment of the juveniles whom haven't been taught that irreparable harm is inflict on those they bully. Many as they grew older realize they had shamed themselves all could be eliminated if parents would instill the concept of love thy neighbors as thyself to their children.

Raymond Paul Boyd

Printed in the United States
by Baker & Taylor Publisher Services